Copyr

A. ~~rights reserved~~

ISBN: 9798316889044

Cover design by: R.J. Powell; Myles Murphy
Library of Congress Control Number: 2018675309
Printed in the United States of America

CONTENTS

PUPPET

R.J. Powell

TRIGGER WARNING

This is a book of **extreme horror**.

Some content may be upsetting.

Reader discretion is strongly advised.

ONE

The blisters surrounding Miss Teacher's vaginal entrance were beginning to leak fluid, mixing with her internal juices.

Squish.

Squish.

Squish.

She placed her hands on her knees to help widen her hips. "Get your hand in there, boy. Get those Skittles out of me!" she harped, her raspy voice reverberating off the paneling of the old kitchen.

Charlie's arm ached. He despised being poor and always having to stay late at Miss Teacher's house. His dad works so hard for him, but he has no idea what really goes on when it's late.

Looking up between her legs, he squinted in the setting sun that shined in from a cigarette smoke-stained window. The yellow of the glass accentuated the glow of the twilight. "Please, can I stop? My arm hurts and I think I got them all." A glint of hope crossed his eyes. Charlie looked down at his arm as it was still inside the old woman, a sticky mess.

Miss Teacher lifted her head and gazed down at him. "I'm almost done," she moaned in between heavy breaths.

As the motions continued. Charlie's mind went to back when his mother was alive. Back before she got sick and needed the special tubes. The methodic movement of his muscles sent his memory into a state of hypnotic overdrive; laughter, swingsets, and racecars repeating like films on an old reel.

It wasn't long until he was done. He knew he had retrieved all of the candy long ago, but Miss Teacher didn't like it when he didn't make her call his name, for some reason. He never understood why someone would want to make those sounds willingly as if she was happy to be in pain.

"May I go wash up, now?" he asked politely, his arm already

beginning to crust over.

Miss Teacher gently closed her legs, careful not to pop any of the remaining blisters. Her hole leaked red and green fluid from the Skittles' sugary coating that was still lodged deep within her canal.

"Yes," she replied callously. "Hurry up and get back here when you're done. I got one more thing for ya to do." She pulled her dress down, letting it fall to her ashy ankles as Charlie trailed off to the restroom down the hall holding his arm out to the side, careful not to catch a waft of the smell.

He hated making her moan like that, but the absolute worst part of it all was the smell. His hand always smelled the worst. One time, she forced him to keep it inside her for so long that his fingers turned into tiny little prunes. His dad worked extra late that evening, so when he retrieved his hand, it was so hot, wet, and pruney. When they got home, dad didn't even let him take a bath because it was too late so Charlie had to sleep with pussy rot on his extremity.

Charlie passed the playroom on his route, stopping in his tracks before checking behind him to make sure the coast was clear. He knew the playroom was off-limits after the rest of the children went home.

Sauntering in quietly, he tip-toed across the room, the floorboards of the near-condemned house creaking beneath his small weight. Bending over, Charlie quietly picked up his favorite doll.

"I wish I could take you home with me," Charlie whispered, running his sticky fingers across the doll's pursed lips. Its blue eyes shimmered behind the dust that gently fell in the darkness of the room.

A brief memory of Charlie's mother came flooding to him. His favorite memory; he was just three years old when his mother gave him a similar doll for Christmas. She cried when she saw his face light up like a tree. Charlie looked up at his mother, tears streaming down her cheeks as he gently took his tiny hand and wiped them away. "It's okay, Mama," he whispered to her as she held him. "I'm happy."

A tear fell from Charlie's eye

landing on the cheek of the plastic doll. It rolled down into its mouth before Charlie had a chance to wipe it away with his sleeve.

"You about done back there?" called Miss Teacher from the kitchen. Charlie heard water running and quickly dropped the doll before heading to the restroom. He splashed soap and water up his entire arm, wetting the floor of the bathroom. After drying his hands, Charlie hung the towel back on the rack and scurried down the hallway toward the kitchen.

"Ma'am?" he said.

"What was taking you so long, boy?"

Charlie looked away, eyeing the

rug under the kitchen table that had wet droplets from the prior event. "Oh, I don't know."

"I need you to clean me up," she said, placing a towel under the warm water. "My sores are actin' up and I need my medicine on it." Pulling her skirt back up, she hiked her leg on the kitchen chair while balancing her upper body weight against the counter. With one arm, she spread her buttocks. The smell was still ripe; a mixture of rotten onions and feces rising through the air mixing with the smell of cigarette smoke. Her grey pubic hair was stuck together in sticky clumps all around her blisters. Charlie gagged. She lit a cigarette.

❊ ❊ ❊

The tear from Charlie penetrated the fibers of the plastic, making its way throughout the doll. Its fingertips slowly moved, then its wrist, and little by little the doll quietly came to life.

Beneath the swirl of the dust, peaking through the stained window, the tiny boy blinked.

"Ahem," he said, clearing his throat, the inside sticking together like dried molasses. "I can speak." His voice was tender and sweet, the way a voice would sound if a marshmallow could speak.

A grin crept across the lively doll's face until he heard the moaning from the kitchen, catching him off guard. His head turned abruptly, the blue hair of his eyebrows furrowed. *Hmm,* he mumbled to himself. *I wonder what that could be.* The boy's saddened face turned upwards into curiosity.

The little doll tip-toed down the hallway, his tiny plastic blue shoes barely coming in contact with the linoleum.

"Yes, right there Charlie. Rub in the ointment," said the old woman. The doll peeked his head around the corner of the wall before he eyed a set of rolling pins on the counter.

"I've got it all," said Charlie.

Miss Teacher hiked her leg up further. "Get in there, boy!" she harked. "Put it on the special blister at the top. Rub it *real* good."

Charlie continued rubbing when he saw something out of the corner of his eye. He turned quickly, but whatever it was had disappeared behind the island counter. "There's ... there's someone here?"

"What are you talki--," Suddenly, she was cut off. Charlie watched in slow motion as Miss Teacher's head leaned forward then went crashing backward as a rolling pin met her skull. The old woman slumped over and slinked to the kitchen floor, behind her revealing a small child standing on the kitchen counter.

"Wh-- who are... are you?" stammered Charlie, his gaze locked in a trance on the strange-looking tiny tot. Charlie took a step back.

"Oh, hi Charlie," he replied. "I'm Puppet." A smile stretched in a cartoonish way from ear to ear as his bright blue eyes gleamed, matching the ocean-colored tuft of hair that set gently atop his head. "You know me, Charlie. *You* call me Pip."

"But how are you ..."

"Alive?"

Charlie nodded.

"I'm not sure. Magic, I guess."

"What are you doing here?"

"I suppose I'm here to help you."

Charlie glanced at the old

12

woman slumped against the kitchen counter, her ankle-length dress twisted around her legs. Charlie felt his throat constrict. "With her?"

Puppet shrugged, another grin shooting across his face. "How old are you, Charlie?" he asked.

"Six. Why?"

"You're a big, strong six-year-old, aren't you, Charlie?"

He looked at his feet and shrugged. "I guess."

Puppet hopped down from the counter, his plastic shoes landing with tiny taps. Looking up at Charlie, he chuckled to himself before taking on a look of shyness. "Let's play a game."

"I'm tired of games, Pip. I just wanna go home."

"When is your dad gonna be here?"

"A long time after dark."

"Then we may have time for a few games," he smiled. "Don't worry, kiddo. They'll be fun."

TWO

The old woman lay nude on the kitchen table, her head falling to the side as she drooled in her slumber of head trauma. It pooled on the wood beneath her cheek while jump ropes held her hands and legs down in place.

"Now what," asked Charlie timidly.

"What do you wanna do?"

Charlie laughed, "let's poop on her!"

Pip giggled, "That's a good one.

What else?"

"We could turn her into someone like you," he said.

Confusion swept across Pip's face. "What do you mean?"

"Ya know, like a puppet!"

"Oh, I like this idea. Pip made his way around the table, his little legs carrying him quicker than one would anticipate. After three tiny hops on chairs, he stood tall next to Miss Teacher's limp body. "What does she do to you?" he asked as he looked down at her.

Charlie looked away, his inquisitive expression quickly fading. "She makes me take things out of her."

Pip sighed, carefully choosing his next words. He walked to Miss

Teacher's mouth further, letting his turd slide down and across her tongue.

She stirred, chewing, then began to swallow.

The smell of the shit hot on her breath swirled through the air of the kitchen.

"Wakey wakey," whispered Puppet as he poked her face.

The old woman gagged once more before instinctively beginning to chew on the shit.

"What..." she grumbled, a sliver of brown liquid running down her lips. "What's happening." Her breath lit up the room; a mixture of feces and rot.

"You're gonna play a game with us!" shouted Puppet. He bent down next to her ear. "I shit in your mouth," he whispered, smiling. "It was Charlie's idea."

Gagging, the old woman tilted her head to the side and immediately began to vomit. Orange and brown chunks spewed from her onto her shoulder, the smell filling the air once more.

"Yuck," said Charlie, looking away.

"What did *I* do to *you*? " she shouted. "Who even *are* you and why are you in *my house*?!"

Puppet stood tall, towering over his new plaything. His smile faded fast. "You don't know who I am?" he asked, quietly, as if saddened by the revelation.

The old woman stared in silence before shaking her head. "No! Of course not! I run a bona-fide business here! An in-home daycare, full of children. Happy children! Untie me!" she yelled.

Pip stood silent before slowly opening his mouth.

"Every little boy you diddled, I was there standing watch. Every tear that fell, asking you to stop, I was there." Pip bent down once more. "And today ... every time you cry, it's just gonna hurt even more," he whispered.

Tears welled up in the old woman's eyes as fear stretched across her wrinkled skin. "Fuck you," she grumbled. Her breasts sagged down her ribs, rising and falling with each labored breath. Brown nipples, cracked and large, accentuated her flaps of mammary tissue.

With his gaze never breaking from hers, Puppet called out from over his shoulder. "Hey Charlie, can you go get the Legos?" Charlie immediately darted off to the playroom, his heavy footsteps pattering quickly down the hallway before reappearing, holding an enlarged bag of tiny toys.

"Perfect," said Puppet. "Just put them there," he nodded toward the end of the table.

Puppet stood in between Miss Teacher's opened legs. "You like putting things inside your pussy, right?"

"Oh, shut the fuck up. You don't know anything. You're a *child*," Miss

Teacher hissed.

Puppet paused. He glared at the woman.

"You're worse than a child. You don't even exist in real life," she hissed once more.

Pip didn't move. He continued to stare. "Charlie, go get a knife," he demanded, his gaze unwavering. He waited patiently for Charlie to retrieve the blade from the counter, placing it directly in his tiny hand.

"Thank you, Dollface," Pip smiled at the young boy before turning back to the old woman. Looking down at the knife, the sliver glistened under the orange hue of the yellow bulbs.

"What're you gonna do with

that?" she said.

"I'm gonna play teacher!" He moved in between her legs, straddling the left one. With the knife in his hand, he held her big toe with his other hand. "It's time to teach you a lesson."

"Get the *fuck* off me, you little shit," she kicked, her legs unmoving by the restraint of the jump rope. "You're not even real!"

Spreading her toes apart, Pip placed the blade against the tender flesh between the two toes. With slight pressure and a quick swish of his wrist, the blade sliced through the tendons and muscles of the sensitive area.

Miss Teacher howled, her rasp

coming through in sharp spurts. Her legs continued to kick as blood pooled beneath her foot. The shit stench from her hot breath filled the room once more, mixing with a slight metalllic undertone.

"Nooo!!!" she tried to kick,

Without flinching, Pip moved to the next toe, slicing in between the two. He smiled as the blade made contact with his wailing victim.

"Stop moving so much; it'll go quicker," he complained, wincing at the blood gathering next to his shoes. He quickly sliced the next, and the next, before moving to her left foot. Taking the heel into his hand, he ran the blade directly through her Achilles tendon, slicing it in half. The muscles hung freely as blood began to gush beneath her.

The screams didn't let up. Gasping in between breaths, her cries shook the table at the base, rocking it against the chipped linoleum of the kitchen floor.

Puppet stood tall, admiring his handiwork and smiling proudly. Looking at Charlie with delight, he noticed the events had painted the boy's face chagrin.

"What's wrong?" asked Pip, hopping down from the table. Miss Teacher continued to sob behind him.

"That was scary," said Charlie.

"What was so scary about it?"

"You." Charlie looked at his feet as immediate shame overtook him.

Puppet lifted his chin. "I'm sorry, kiddo. I didn't mean to scare ya."

The two locked eyes, and for a moment, Charlie felt the anger that was consuming Puppet. Charlie had been subjected to Miss Teacher's tricks for far too long. He couldn't imagine all of the scenarios that Puppet had witnessed.

Charlie furrowed his brow, his face contorting to that of an angry child. "Okay, Pip. Let's play before Daddy comes to get me."

The corners of Pip's mouth lifted, spreading slowly in a caricature-like way as a devilish smile crept across his face.

Miss Teacher stared at the two in horror, terrified of what a doll could possibly be capable of.

THREE

"Holy shit, it's a crab buffet down here," exclaimed Pip. He examined the pubic area of the old woman. "Fascinating infrastructure you've got here, ma'am." Pip ran his finger up her slit, opening it and revealing cottage-like cheese oozing from her folds. A fishy smell arose through the air.

"Please," she cried. "Please stop."

"Yeah, that's what they all said." He began moving his hand in and out of her. Chunks of smegma built up on his knuckles. "Whew. You're ripe!"

Charlie couldn't help but look away as the small doll raped the old woman with his fist.

"You like that, don't you, or do you prefer it when the boys cry?. Hey Charlie," he called out from over his shoulder. "What's your favorite game to play here?"

"Sometimes she lets us play Scrabble with her."

"Done. Let's play some Scrabble!"

Charlie stood, still keeping his gaze away from the old woman's gaping hole, and retrieved the items from the playroom. "Here ya go," he said, handing the bag of tiles to Pip.

The Lego's sat next to her left leg.

"Thanks, buddy!" Pip gleefully cheered before he took the bag, retrieving a small tile in his tiny hand. "The letter C for *cheese vapors* - the smell of your cunt." Without hesitation, Pip plunged the smile tile in the old woman's hole, the edges of the wooden square scraping against her vaginal walls. She screamed and tried to close her legs to no avail.

Charlie grinned. "Do another," he said.

Pip reached into the bag once more, this time pulling out the letter G. He used his other hand to spread her lips this time, exposing her elongated clitoris; it pulsated at the cold air. Around it were dollops of hardened cream that had dried to her skin. The smell was putrid, rising fast through Pip's small nostrils.

"Jesus, do you ever bathe?" he asked. "Letter G for *gunk flaps*." He angled the tile to the side before shoving it inside the woman's birth canal. She shrieked as the corners of the wood scraped along her internal walls before being driven directly into her cervix.

Pip reached for another tile.

"Please," she said.

Pausing, "please what?" he replied.

"Please stop."

He stared, his expression unreadable.

"The letter P for *pus gullet* -

used in a sentence: I don't know what this means, but it sounds fitting for a *pus gullet* such as yourself," he said. Without pause, Pip drove his hand deep inside the old woman, the tiles building up at her cervix. Each one pressed its sharp edges into her fleshy interior, driving the pain through her organs.

"Please, just fucking stop!" she pleaded with Pip.

"Fine," he digressed. "But I have to use the Lego's too; can't leave anything to waste."

He slowly shoved each Lego inside her before pausing. What're these other holes?" he asked as his eyes peered between the tufts of grey hair.

Charlie appeared next to the

table. "I'm not sure what the little one is. She just makes me put things in the big one."

"It's my fuckin' piss hole, you idiots," barked the old woman. The two boys looked at each other, Charlie, grimacing, as a smile slowly began to appear across Pip's face.

Realization tore through the old woman's eyes. "No," she pleaded before shaking her head. "You can't."

"Oh, but I can. And I *will*," slighted Pip, an ache for more coursing through his newly formed veins. He took his fingers and spread her lips, opening them wide as he gazed at the inner workings of the female anatomy. With a tile in his hand, he worked the corner against her urethra, doing his best to make it fit. The old woman constantly squirmed, yelling for Pip to stop.

"Owwwww!"

"I need something smaller," he realized, looking at Charlie. The two stayed locked on before Pip had a thought. He peered up and in between Miss Teacher's legs. "Hey, remember that time you denied Carson his insulin until he removed all the friendship beads from your dusty cave?"

"He deserved it!" she called out as Pip jumped down from the table, scurrying down the hall. "The little shit pissed on the bathroom wall!"

It wasn't long until he returned wielding a small, white box. Pip opened it revealing a tiny syringe. In his other hand, he had a bottle of water. "Let's see what this does."

The old woman yelped and attempted to squeeze her knees together to no avail.

"The more you move, the worse it'll be," Pip warned.

Charlie shielded his eyes; he couldn't watch.

Pip removed the cap from the syringe and sunk it into the bottle of water, quickly filling it up. He opened her lips once more revealing a small hole. Pip pressed the needle inside it, spreading her wrinkled lips further as he went. The needle would catch against a urethral wall sending the old woman into a fit of rage.

"Ahhhhh!" She screamed behind

her tears, a cacophony of pleas and anger.

He pressed his thumb against the end, pushing down as the cool water exited the syringe and shot up her urethra. She screamed once more as the liquid filled her up.

Pip laughed; Charlie grimaced behind his hands.

"We need something stronger than water," said Pip.

The woman shook her head. "Please! I can't take it anymore!" she shouted.

Pip paused where he stood. He eyed her mysteriously. "You can't?"

"No, Puppet." Her sobs were infrequent while snot hung from her nose, swaying with her movements and occasionally sticking to her upper lip. Pip recalled all those times when the children complained about their arms being tired, or their necks being sore. He thought about them asking for water after and her denying their basic needs. "Please," she begged. "Please stop."

His chest felt tight; something he hadn't experienced yet - a feeling of remorse and regret. Pip turned to look at Charlie who could do nothing but simply shrug.

"No," he said.

She stopped crying and looked at him straight on, raising her head from the hard top of the table. "No?" she said, in her *try me* teacher voice.

"No. Don't ask again - isn't that

what *you* always say?"

"Fuck you, pipsqueak."

He laughed. "That's a good one, Blister Betty."

The two continued staring at each other until Pip went to the kitchen sink and retrieved a small, white bottle with the words *bleach* in big bold, blue letters across the front. He hopped back onto the table, retrieved the syringe, and dunked it into the bottle.

"No!" she screamed, attempting to flail her arms.

He suctioned the bleach into the syringe, overwhelming the room in its aroma.

Pip spread her lips once more so that her urethra could be completely exposed to the cool air. It was red and swollen from its previous sodomization.

He inserted the needle into her pisshole and squeezed the end, injecting the entire syringe full of bleach directly inside her. She screamed, her gasps filling the room with her hot, shit breath that mixed with the stinging smell of the chemical. Her body started to convulse on the table while her screams were the sentiment of death as an out.

"Just kill me," she pleaded, sobbing and breathless. "Please, just kill me."

Pip relaxed in between her legs as he watched blood trickle from her sensitive areas. Her furrowed lips twitched in between her continued sobs.

"Shall we break for lunch?" asked Pip.

"Umm, I think it's like 18 p.m." replied Charlie.

"Close. It's six, which is dinner time. Why don't you whip us up something to eat?"

"Sure thing, pal."

Pip moved closer to Miss Teacher's face. The old woman flinched.

"It hurts, Puppet. Please," she asked quietly. "Please, just end me and I won't be around anymore to do anything again."

"So, you *know* how wrong it is?"

"Well, I mean, it's illegal." She

rolled her eyes.

"Do you know how many little boys' lives you ruined forever?"

Her silence was paramount as tears poured down her cheeks. Her thighs trembled the table in small, infrequent earthquakes. Miss Teacher looked at the darkened ceiling, tracing the circles of stained cigarette smoke rings with her eyes.

"Seventeen."

She continued to look away.

"Seventeen little boys you ruined. Do you understand that?"

Rolling her eyes once more, she finally turned to face him. "Listen, you fucking play thing. Every single one of those boys deserved it," she hissed. "Every single one of them needed to be taught a lesson for the shit they pull in my fucking daycare."

"Like Charlie?!" he quipped, pointing to the small boy on the other side of the room. Charlie was standing in the kitchen with a loaf of bread and the makings of a peanut butter and jelly sandwich. He held a butterknife in his hand as he swirled the brown mixture onto the bread.

"Charlie's different," she said, a softness in her tone.

Silence overtook the room. "What do you mean *different*?"

"He doesn't cry."

The two continued watching Charlie work his way with the jelly, now, his knife weaving over the bread as if he were casting a magic spell.

Pip watched on in compassion and empathy for a child subjected to such horrors. Miss Teacher watched on for other reasons.

FOUR

The two sat quietly on the floor, eating their peanut butter and jelly sandwiches. They could hear the raspy breathing of the old woman lying strewn across the kitchen table.

"I can smell that, ya know."

"Good," piped Pip with a mouth full of the sugary concoction. They chewed, scarfing down the remnants of their dinner. The sun had fully set behind the trees outside as an orange hue came and went.

The boys washed down the sandwiches with juice boxes from the fridge. "This is delicious!" harped Pip, having never had juice before. His taste buds were throwing parties on his tongue.

"What next?" asked Charlie, wiping the jam from the corner of his mouth with his arm.

Pip smiled, thinking to himself. "Hmm," he murmured. "What's your favorite game she lets you play?"

"Oh! One time we played *don't crack the egg.* That was so much fun 'cause Suzy ran off–"

"Lightbulb," Pip cut in.

"Huh?"

"I have an idea."

"What's the idea?"

Moments later, Charlie returned to the kitchen holding a round, white object per the request from his new friend. He handed it to Pip as the toy-like boy leaped back up onto the table.

"You liked playing *don't crack the egg* with them, huh?" Pip asked the old woman.

She stared blankly at him.

"I have an idea for a new game," he said. "This one's called *don't crack the lightbulb*."

The woman's face flushed, turning to pale white. "No," she said. "You can't!"

He smiled.

Pip spread the woman's vaginal lips once more, revealing her gaping hole. He placed the metal end cap of the bulb against her opening and pushed it inside slowly. Crusts of blood surrounded her vulva, breaking free and floating down onto the wooden table like flecks of paprika. Her blisters had yellowed and pus began to leak against the pressure inside her.

"Please! Please, don't go any further!"

Pip paused, as if to consider her request, before smiling and pushing the the bulb in further. The insides rattled metallic as her hips bounced. "Listen, lady, the point of this game is to *not* break the bulb inside you." Her hips came to a freeze as the lightbulb was pushed in further. Millimeter by millimeter, Pip worked its way beyond her initial vaginal muscles and deep inside her pussy.

"Atta girl," he said. "Almost there." He held his tongue out of his mouth as her lips folded around the glass. Her vagina, loose and wet, allowed the bulb to enter with ease.

"There!" Pip shouted, standing straight with his hands on his hips. "How does that feel?"

"Ffffuuuck ... yoehhh," she breathlessly whispered in an attempt not to use any abdominal muscles.

"Mmmm, no thanks," he replied.

"Now what?" asked Charlie from the kitchen floor. He sat with another empty juice box in his lap.

"I bet Pustule Princss is hungry?" asked Pip.

"Yes," she whispered once more. "Please, get- this - out of me."

"Only after you eat. Charlie, wanna make her a sandwich?"

"Sure! PB and J?"

"You betcha," smiled Pip.

As Charlie made his way around the kitchen once more, Pip walked towards the woman's head. He slowly bent down, his sullen face turning upwards into a catastrophically evil grin. "You're gonna love this."

As Charlie approached with the sandwich, Pip's face reverted to his depressive expression. "Thank you, pal. Can you also toss me a butterknife, perchance?"

Charlie opened a kitchen drawer before handing it to the young boy. "Here ya go," he said.

Pip smiled from ear to ear. "Let's see how this pans out." Pip removed the two pieces of bread from one another and set them on the table next to the woman. He then spread her buttocks revealing a grey, hairy asshole that pucked at his sight. Placing the tip of the butterknife against her asshole, he slowly began to insert it, ridged side facing up.

"Let's see what happens when I do…" he gave the knife a shove. "This."

The woman screamed out in pain as the small, metal knife was inserted into her posterior, it's ridges forcing painful intrusions against the

PUPPET

wall of her anal cavity. The metal raked against the glass with nothing but a simple piece of skin separating the two.

"Aooooohhhhhh," she screamed, sucking in her stomach as if to not flinch anything else. Her focus solely relied on that of her vagina, to not break the bulb.

Pip angled the knife downwards and removed it revealing globs of feces on the end of the stainless steel utensil. He picked up the piece of bread with the peanut butter and began smearing the shit into it. The chunky, dark brown turds mixed with ease in the nutty butter.

The woman continued to let out a chorus of whimpering cries as she tried tirelessly to not break the bulb.

Charlie sat on the floor wide-eyed.

"Mama always said if the butterknife comes out dirty, it's still cookin'," he said with a smile.

Pip inserted the knife once more, scooping out another glob of shit. A brown-stained corn kernel was wedged into the end of the excrement. It weaved onto the piece of bread resembling a decadent chocolate-peanut butter spread. The corn kernel was quickly covered, hidden amongst the nuts.

Pip continued moving the knife in and out of the old woman's asshole. grey pubic hair caught in the midst leveled easily onto the sandwich, the ends of each hair glistening from the dried blood. Each weave of dark chocolate shit set another layer on top of the light brown mixture.

Like a fresh rain of the season in the scorching African savanna, mud mixed with sand. The knife, a paintbrush among the landscape as howls of animal-like creatures echoed off in the distance. A celebration of prosperity.

Pip inserted the knife once more.

Suddenly, there was a crack.

The woman gasped, sucking in her stomach and trying with every fiber of her muscles to not break the bulb.

The room was still.

Silent.

Crack.

Pip turned his head slowly to look at Charlie. His eyes were wide, the whites of them glistening under the dim kitchen light.

Pip looked up at Miss Teacher.

Pop.

Her eyes were nearly bulging before the scream let out, an obvious reminder that hell exists. Her raspy voice reverberated off the stained walls of the kitchen

The bulb had burst inside her, its glass shards springing to life with nowhere to go but outwards against her walls. Her pussy immediately started to convulse blood, sending it pouring down her opened hole and streaming across the puckering ridges of her hairy asshole.

The glass penetrated everything. The *Scrabble* tiles and *Lego* pieces that remained shoved against her cervix had dislodged slightly, only to be replaced by thin sheets of tiny knives. Her screams were a chorus of demonic rage as she slowly began to dissociate. The glass penetrated the wall of her anal cavity, pushing droplets of blood out of her asshole.

Pip looked at Charlie once more. "Whoops," he shrugged under the umbrella of cries. Her hips bucked as her legs rocked back and forth. Miss Teacher wanted nothing more than to shut them, but she couldn't; they were tied down with great strength to the table.

The two boys stood silently, one

on the floor and the other on the table as they watched the old woman writhe.

"Is she gonna die," asked Charlie.

Pip couldn't answer. Not that he didn't want to, but that he wasn't sure.

The screams ended abruptly as the old woman finally passed out from the intensity of the pain.

"Not yet," replied Pip.

FIVE

"What hap– happened…" she croaked out like a toad on the asphalt of a Texas summer parking lot, the rasp exacerbated after the excessive screaming episode.

"You died," said Charlie, bewilderment sweeping across his face.

"No, you didn't, but close," replied Pip. "We still have some playing to do."

A heavy sigh could be heard coming from her chest as it slowly rattled.

"You hungry?" asked Pip. The old woman nodded as he made his way next to her head. His sky-blue eyes met hers as she watched him slowly. He unwrapped the sandwich from a paper towel and began feeding it to her.

"How does that taste?"

"Mmm," she chewed. "It's okay."

Pip continued feeding her the *Poo PB and J*, as Charlie so eloquently called it while she was unconscious. They had a long talk about his home life, his mother, and his favorites, at which point Charlie confessed that after the "Poo PB and J" incident, he doesn't think he'd want more in the near future. Pip understood.

It didn't take the woman long until she had scarfed down the entire sandwich. Pip assumed she was so focused on the objects in her vagina, she just completely disregarded the sandwich altogether as it was happening.

"How's that bat cave feel?" he asked.

"Hurts, Pip. It fucking hurts and I need a hospital."

"Well, I need you to stop being a

pedophile, and then we could talk."

"I never *hurt* those boys!" she screamed, her head lifting from the table as her grey curls fell by the side. "All I did was put them to work from time to time. They all grew up and moved on with their lives, and *you should, too!*" She hissed, shitty spit flinging from her lips. Remnants of the brown peanut butter turd-wich had coated her tongue in a thick film.

Pip couldn't do anything but stand in silence, his blank expression staring heartlessly at her as she used all her strength to spew vitriol in his direction.

"Do you smell that?" he asked.

"And then you have the unmitigated gall to hold me hostage in my *own* daycare that I run in my own ho–"

Pip's foot landed with a loud thud against her jaw. "Please be quiet while I think," he said.

She spat blood, droplets trickling down her chin. "Jesus, do you smell that?"

he requested once more. "It smells …" Pip sniffed the air, the blue freckles that dotted his nose crinkled. "It smells *putrid; rotten.*"

Sniff, sniff.

It led him to her vagina.

He immediately jerked back.

"Like my nana's farts after she eats breakfast," giggled Charlie.

"You must have an infection inside there. Charlie, grab me a razor blade, please."

"Sure thing, pal!" he said before running to the bathroom. Within seconds, Charlie returned holding a small pink razor with rusted blades.

Miss Teacher coughed, blood spewing from her mouth.

"Quickly," shouted Pip. "She can't die yet. Not until the finale!"

Charlie handed Pip the razor.

"Thanks. I also need something to

clean her with."

As Charlie made his way around the daycare looking for the items requested, Pip ran the blade horizontally down the old woman's lips. The dry blade pricked every pubic hair, pulling each one from the root.

Miss Teacher barely flinched when the blade met the first blister. It was still sealed despite the trauma, and fluid moved beneath the surface. "Awe," cooed Pip. "They're like tiny waterbeds for crabs." The rusty blade nicked the pus-filled blister before popping, sending a yellow substance trickling down her grey hairs. The blade continued, sweeping up the hair in swift, harsh motions.

Charlie reappeared. "Will this work? Her blister medicine and a bottle of … uhh – I'm not sure. I can't read."

"Perfect!" shouted Pip from the table. He watched the skinny tube fly through the air toward him, landing with a thud on his hand holding the razor. It shifted to its side and sliced a portion of

Miss Teacer's labia minora off.

She screeched, an onslaught of burning wheels coming to a stop. Her voice penetrated the air around them like nails on a chalkboard as sweat and blood began to build up around her remaining folds.

Pip grimaced; his eyes looking away from the gushing pussy lip. "Let me clean you up."

He reached for the metal tube and flipped it on its side. *Lysol.*

Pip aimed it at her open wound and squeezed the top releasing a spray of disinfectant directly into the open blisters and gash. Her agonizing screams echoed down the darkened hallway of the house and they didn't stop.

"Fuuuck," she called out. "Pleaaaseee, stopppp!"

"Oh, does that hurt?" he asked, seemingly shocked. With the can still in his hand, he pressed the top of the spray tube against Miss Teacher's vaginal opening. Her muscles spread easily as the metal bypassed her entrance, pressing the glass shard deeper into her skin as he pushed on. The tube stretched her out before coming to a stop.

"I can't do it anymore!" she screamed.

Pip pressed the Lysol can's end with his fist. He used all his strength, but something was blocking the tube from entering her completely.

"It hurts!!"

He hopped down from the table and stood quietly in the kitchen, observing his surroundings. All around him were screams of agony.

In the darkened corner, leaned against the wall was a broom covered in cobwebs. There was no telling when the last time it had been used was. He retrieved the wooden stick, dragging it across the floor as he made his way back to the table.

Pip positioned himself in between

her legs with the wooden broomstick in his hands. He pressed the end of it against the tube before pulling it backward and giving it a hard *WHACK.* The can was met with a metallic thud just as another howl was let out from Miss Teacher.

Hmm, he thought. Pip stood back and held the broomstick tighter. With one more loud thud, he slammed it into the can of Lysol as hard as he could, and with that, the *Scrabble* and *Lego* pieces burst through her cervix. The can shoved deeper down inside her.

With the broomstick still in hand, he gave it one final shove as her moist hole swallowed the can all together, ripping directly through her cervix and impaling her uterus.

Gasp.

Her stomach sank as she took in a gulp of air. Suddenly, there was just silence while her screams stopped completely.

Charlie wrestled with what was

happening. The scene in front of him, his nude teacher law strewn across her kitchen table, her insides brutalized so badly; stuffed like a puppet on a stick. He watched her stomach slowly rise and fall.

"Hey," asked Pip from in between her legs. Nothing.

"Miss Teacher?" asked Charlie. He walked to the table and stared sadly at the empty expression that had swept her face.

Pip stood and quickly hopped over her leg. He watched her move slowly while looking down at her sunken face. The broomstick still hung from inside her. "You alive?" he asked.

Suddenly, another gasp of air occurred as she quickly sat her head up, leaning to the side and using her teeth to sink into Pip's pale, little leg.

"Owwwww, you bitch!" he shrieked, sending his other leg flying forward and landing with a wet thud against her cheek, causing her to unclench her jaw. Tattered bite marks stained his skin pink.

Charlie jumped back from the table before falling to the floor. "You okay?" he called out.

"Yeah, I'll be fine, Charlie. But can you grab a pair of scissors?"

Charlie disappeared down the hallway while Pip sat quietly in between her legs waiting for the return of his friend. After a few moments, a pair of gardening sheers had graced his tiny hand. "No childproof ones?" he asked.

Charlie shrugged and smiled before taking a seat in the kitchen chair.

Pip sat quietly as he went to work. "This game is called *it's almost over.*"

With his fingers pinching her left set of lips, he pulled them outwards and angled the sharp metal downward. He lined the cheesy flesh perfectly in between the two blades and slowly began squeezing it. Pip watched as the metal first pinched, then began to cut the flesh wide open while blood poured down her buttocks. Little by little, the old woman's hairy lip separated from her body and finally fell to the floor leaving behind a gash of a red river flowing in its wake.

She could barely scream at this point, but Pip could see the pain in the earthquakes that were her thighs. He moved the scissors to the other lip and removed it completely. Pip sat up, admiring his handiwork. On each side were flattened holes where flesh once was while in the middle a set of loose skin, untouched by pain, hung freely.

Pip placed his little pointer finger and thumb on each side of her clitoris and pulled outwards. With a quick snip of the scissors, it was gone. He held it up, examining the tiny fleshy bead. "Interesting," he said.

Gasp.

A murmur fled.

Holding her internal lips outward, he positioned the scissors around them once more and quickly squeezed, sending the wrinkled skin dropping to the blood-soaked table.

"Look at *that*," he said, standing up. Pip placed his hands on his hips and smiled. Before him was a religious-like image. A nude lady, extremities extended, her reproductive organs impaled and her womanhood removed. A pool of blood spread beneath her as her vagina stretched open, the broomstick rising and falling with each labored breath.

"I call this *The Marionette's Lament*."

SIX

The sound of a swirling machine sent shivers down her spine. Pain radiated deep within her as her body shook in a steady wave of unrelenting quakes. Shock took hold, and she could feel herself beginning to fade.

"Not so fast," said a small voice. "Drink this."

Cold glass pressed firmly against her lips while a hand helped lift her head. Her tongue moved in motion as a warm, thick liquid made contact with her tongue. She swallowed, having never tasted such a thing before. It was meaty, like ground-up steak that hadn't been cooked. Metallic, copper. She couldn't quite make it out but didn't have the stamina to tell her captor *no*.

"How does that cunt slushie taste," the voice whispered in her ear.

Her eyes slowly opened as she realized what was happening. The cool air could be felt all around her groin; exposed, but radiating a feverish heat. Her lips were gone and she just drank them.

Pip bent over and began to whisper in her ear. "Before you go, I just wanted you to know that it doesn't matter who you are on the outside. A man, a woman, a fucking doll … evil deserves to die regardless."

"Go … to … hell …" she croaked out, a strawberry meat mustache coating her upper lip. Belching, the waft of raw meat filled the air. She breathed heavily before finally whispering back "And I'll see you there."

The old woman's eyes fell to the side as her heart finally stopped beating. The boys glanced at each other before Pip felt his toes begin to tingle.

"You okay?" asked Charlie.

"I, uhh.. I'm not sure. I can't move," he replied.

While Miss Teacher's body gave out, as did Pip's. Charlie couldn't understand what was happening while he watched his first and only friend disappear before his eyes, turning back into a plastic doll. Puppet's face downturned, his expression of sadness overcame him as his baby blue eyes locked onto Charlie's gaze one final time, indefinite time.

* * *

The man sat at his desk, a cigar in hand. All around him were a series of windows that had the blinds drawn shut. The room was dark aside from an overhead lamp. A series of photos of a young boy on a farm were arranged neatly in a row on his desk. The man blew a plume of smoke across the room just as the radio on his desk beeped. "Sarg, the kid said a doll came to life and did it," said the voice, a hopeless tone abundant behind its words.

The man sighed, rubbing his mustache. "Fuck," he whispered. He leaned forward and pressed the button on the receiver. "Where did we send the last one? What was her name?" he said.

"Uhh, Rebecca?"

"Yeah, her."

"We sent her to Hollygrove Asylum," replied the voice.

"What about the doll?"

"She still has it."

"Okay then. Send him there; the boy and the doll. Let them handle it," the man replied.

"Ten-four, Sarg."

ABOUT THE AUTHOR

R.j. Powell

R.J. lives in East Texas with her rottweiler, rat, cat, and amazing children. She spends her downtime reading, writing, gardening, and painting.

She is very active on Instagram and

can be found @splatter.girl or on Tiktok at splattergirlhorror.

Other books by R.J. include Madness in Tandem, Thrice the Madness, Eight Cases of Jane, Dollface, Vasectomy, and her newest palate cleanser, Feeler Deep.

BOOKS IN
THIS SERIES

The Dollhouse
A series of books chronicling dolls that come to life to seek revenge against those who have wronged them.

Dollface

Papa has his victims, but Dollface holds his heart. His perfect little Dolly. Now, she's awake and ready to seek revenge for all she was forced to witness and endure.

TW: Contains SA

NOW AVAILABLE ON AUDIBLE

Printed in Dunstable, United Kingdom

66372870R00051